MW00899609

My Best Friend is Joining the Marine Corps

RICARDO + KONA

Written by Karim Trueblood
Illustrations by Meredith Woods

To my son Ricardo & to Kona

My name is Kona. I am an Alaskan Malamute,
and Ricardo is my best friend.

When Ricardo finished school, he decided to serve our country in the military. He enlisted in the United States Marine Corps.

Everyone was feeling happy and proud.
Ricardo would go on adventures.

But I was feeling worried, I did not know what would happen to my best friend.
Where is he going?
Would I be able to go on these adventures with him?
How long will he be gone?
Is he going to remember me?

As the days came closer to his departure, everything changed. It was evident my best friend was leaving.

I wanted to be with him all the time, but I knew he had a million things to do and places to go. After all, this was the most important adventure and the job of his life.

The day has come, my best friend looked at me with those brown eyes I have been looking at since I was a little puppy, and he said, see you later. I knew by his face it would be a long see you later.

My mom was sad, and my dad was sad, the cats were sad, and the tortoise Coco was sad.
Everyone was sad. I believe they feared not knowing what was happening with my best friend.

But a couple of days later, in the middle of the night, the phone rang, my mom jumped, and she was scared, and happy and proud. I knew she was talking to my brother, my best friend.
I was wagging my tail trying to get to the phone, but it was all too fast.

My best friend's journey in a place they call Parris Island had begun.

They make Marines at Parris Island, so I was scared.
Were they going to replace my best friend?
That would be the only phone call we receive from Ricardo until he becomes a Marine.
Because right now, he is a recruit, and he really wants to be a Marine.
He will only be a Marine after completing some very difficult training for many, many weeks.
I was so concerned about not knowing what would happen.
We waited and waited.

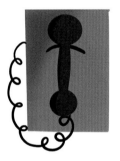

Halloween, without my best friend, was no fun.

One afternoon, a mailman brought a letter from the place where they make Marines. We all were anxiously waiting, and we received encouraging news. My best friend was doing good in his training.

At Parris Island, they feed them well, and they are terribly busy. My best friend's letter sounded uplifting, so we began writing him letters almost every day.

I loved walking to put letters in the mailbox. It was important for him to know how much we love him and support him.

While my best friend was becoming a Marine, I was preparing to be a Marine's best friend. That is not an easy job.

They have a difficult job, and they need their family, friends, and best friends like me to be there for them. It is a team effort. Everyone must help.

Christmas was difficult because I worried about Ricardo. Still, then I remembered he was working to become the person he wanted to be.

I heard that next month he would be graduating from Parris Island, the place where they make Marines.
We get to go there!

Everyone was joyful, his training was going well, and we were encouraged by the idea of seeing him.

The excitement started to shift to graduation preparation.
Everyone, family, and friends alike started to make plans for the big day.

But before my best friend finishes his training, he must pass a final challenge. It is even more challenging than anything any puppy can do. Recruits must work together in the bad weather, with little sleep, and with little food for 54 hours. After they work together and persevere, then they become United States Marines.

My brother was going to enter his final challenge as a recruit. My mom was very concerned, and I kept her company. I knew she needed me. And just like that, we received another call.
My brother, my best friend, called and said, mom, I am a United States Marine!

I was there, I could hear his voice on the phone, I was barking and howling (because I am a snow dog, I like to howl) my mom was happy. People started to hug and cry, filled with gratitude that Ricardo had accomplished his first goal. He was a Marine, and I received extra hugs and rubs that day.

A few weeks later, I was able to travel with my family to see my best friend. It is called family day. Parris Island is intimidating because I knew those people had the very important job of making Marines.

WE MAKE

MARINES

I waited and saw my best friend running with all his Marine friends and then we had a picnic, and it was the best day of my life.
My best friend was happy, and I was proud to see him grow into a Marine.
He is still my absolute best friend and I realized, I had nothing to fear.
Marines are best friends to dogs too.

Ricardo is off to his next adventure, and I always visit him when I can. I know he is working to keep us all safe and protect our country.

I also understand my responsibility of being a Marine's best friend, even if I cannot be with him all the time. I am grateful for my job. I will continue to send pictures and letters to my Marine, until I see him again because I love him.